Pat Hutchins

Greenwillow Books
A DIVISION OF
WILLIAM MORROW & COMPANY, INC.
NEW YORK

Library of Congress Cataloging in Publication Data
Hutchins, Pat (date) Don't forget the bacon!
SUMMARY: A little boy goes grocery shopping for his mother
and tries hard to remember her instructions.
[1. Stories in rhyme]   I.   Title.   PZ8.3.H965Do   [E]
75-17935   ISBN 0-688-80019-X   ISBN 0-688-84019-1 lib. bdg.
ISBN 0-688-06787-5 (1987 Printing)   ISBN 0-688-06788-3 (lib. bdg. 1987 Printing)

For Ben and Jeb Kidd